Dedicated to all of the Little Ruffles of the world who see
the good in the world and find ways to make more of it!

Little Ruffle
and the World Beyond

Written by
Jodie Jackson

Illustrated by
Sarah-Leigh Wills

In a brambly nest above the world
Little Ruffle was tucked up tight.
She couldn't yet see out of her nest
So, relied on others for sight.

The elder birds flew far and wide
to find stories short and long.

And share with Ruffle all that happens
in the world that lies beyond.

Their mission was to keep her safe,
so, they warned of any trouble.
But this made Little Ruffle afraid of the world,
and she stayed tucked up in her bubble.

She didn't want to leave her nest,
the world seemed **big** and **bad**.
The stories that were often told
made Little Ruffle sad.

"I can't look", said Little Ruffle,
as she closed her eyes up tight.

But her Mummy gently
stroked her wing and said:
"My darling it's alright."

"We need to know why the world is sad,
that's why we ask: 'What's the matter?'
But it's no good us just stopping there,
we need to see how it gets better."

"If we want a different story,
we must take a different view.
Climb on, my little darling,
I've got something to show to you."

So Little Ruffle felt her way
to perch upon her mother,

and while her mother flew one way,
Little Ruffle faced the other.

"Now open your eyes", said Mummy,
but Ruffle could manage just one.
Although there may be storms ahead,

The world beneath glowed **big** and **bright**,
Little Ruffle's eye did widen.
For when she looked at the world this way,
she didn't feel so frightened.

You see, in the wake of problems,
something special can be found.
Solutions begin budding,
like little seedlings on the ground.

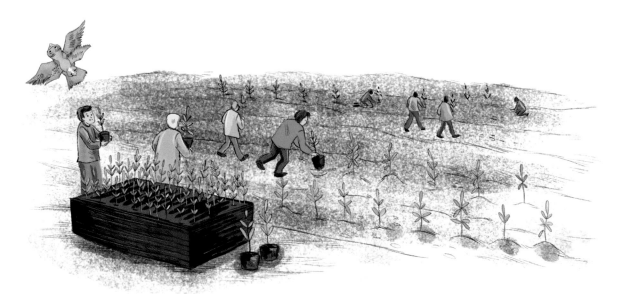

And Little Ruffle kept her gaze
as they swept around in motion.
She watched below as they planted trees
and cleaned up all the ocean.

The problems, they were solvable
by those who dare to try.
But the elders flew too fast to see
and these stories passed them by.

Little Ruffle's heart began to thump
as she watched it from above.
The world seemed so exciting
when she saw it built with love.

They would gather in their gaggles,
they would put their heads together.
They would come up with the answers
that helped make the world feel better.

They would set to work to build a world
more beautiful than before.
Where kindness didn't whisper,
it echoed and it **roared**.

"You see the questions that we ask
will give us answers in return.
And if we ask to see the good,
there's so much we can learn."

But these stories hadn't reached her,
in her treetop way up high
and she thought of all the other birds,
like her, afraid to fly.

Through this eye, Ruffle loved the world.
She asked, "can the other stay shut tight?"

"You need to spread both wings to soar,
and you need two eyes for safe flight."

With that Little Ruffle opened both eyes,
and saw the world in full;
The good and bad sitting side by side
and found she could look at it all.

"I've got to tell the others
of the beauty that I've seen."

"What a good idea my darling,
but you'll have to use those wings"

She thought that she would have to wait
till her wings grew big and strong,

but the strength Ruffle needed to fly the nest
had been with her all along.

Join Little Ruffle on her adventures to see the good in the world by visiting www.littleruffle.co.uk and find engaging activities to help kids become empowered explorers, hopeful heroes and solution seekers!

What happens when kids use Little Ruffle's Resources?

They have higher self-esteem

They have lower levels of anxiety

They become more optimistic and hopeful

They develop active coping

They are more resilient

They have fun

Navigating the news

The elders of our world scour the land to bring us stories of the world beyond – we call it "The News". In an effort to keep us safe, the news reports on all of the problems of the world. But what we don't often hear about is how these problems are being solved and how things might be getting better. This gives an imbalanced picture of the world, where it may seem worse than it is. This can have a harmful impact on our children's, and our own, mental health. But we can navigate the news successfully, not only by being problem finders but also by becoming solution seekers!

If you would like Little Ruffle to report back all of her weekly findings and share the best of the world with you, sign up at www.littleruffle.co.uk and get solutions news straight to your inbox.

About the Author

Jodie Jackson is an expert on the psychological impact of the news and the author of "You Are What You Read: why changing your media diet can change the world". Jodie's research shows that too much bad news is bad for you and shows not only how, but why, including solutions into your media diet has the power to improve your mental health, transform your life, and just possibly change the world.

Follow Little Ruffle @LittleRuffle